This book is dedicated to Nicholas and Manon. RHC

Published by Collins Educational
An imprint of HarperCollins*Publishers* Ltd
77-85 Fulham Palace Road
London W6 8JB

The HarperCollins website address is:
www.**fire**and**water**.com

First published by Letterland Direct Limited, 1994.

This edition published 1998 by Collins Educational
Reprinted 1995, 1996, 1999

ISBN 0 00 303420 8

Printed and bound in the United Kingdom by Scotprint Ltd, Musselburgh, Scotland

Letterland Home Learning

HarperCollins publishes a wide range of Letterland early
learning books, video and audio tapes, puzzles and games.
For an information leaflet about Letterland or to order
materials call 0870 0100 441.

Letterland™

AN ALPHABET OF
RHYMES

Written by RICHARD CARLISLE

Illustrated by KIM RAYMOND and ELIZABETH TURNER

Educational consultant LYN WENDON, originator of LETTERLAND

Collins Educational

An imprint of HarperCollinsPublishers

A
WELCOME
TO
LETTERLAND

"Welcome to Letterland,
we're glad that you've come.
In Letterland everyone
likes to have fun.

Here you'll discover
what's what and who's who.
There's so much to see
and so much to do.

So welcome to Letterland,
we think you'll soon know
some friends you'll remember
wherever you go."

ANNIE APPLE

Our friend Annie Apple climbs high in a tree.
The higher she goes, the more she can see.
She looks for her Letterland friends far below.
She waves as they come, she waves as they go.

BOUNCY BEN

Meet Bouncy Ben, a bouncy bunny.
Here he comes. Isn't he funny?
He'll bounce in the air and bounce on the floor.
Sometimes he'll even bounce through the door!

CLEVER CAT'S CUDDLES

Clever cat likes cuddles
she purrs because it pleases,

unless her nose is tickled
and then she softly sneezes.

DIPPY DUCK'S SONG

One, two, three, four, five
Dippy Duck likes to dive.

Six, seven, eight, nine, ten
Dippy Duck pops up again.

Dippy's going up and down
Dippy's going round and round.

I wonder where did Dippy go?
Now she's tickling your big toe!

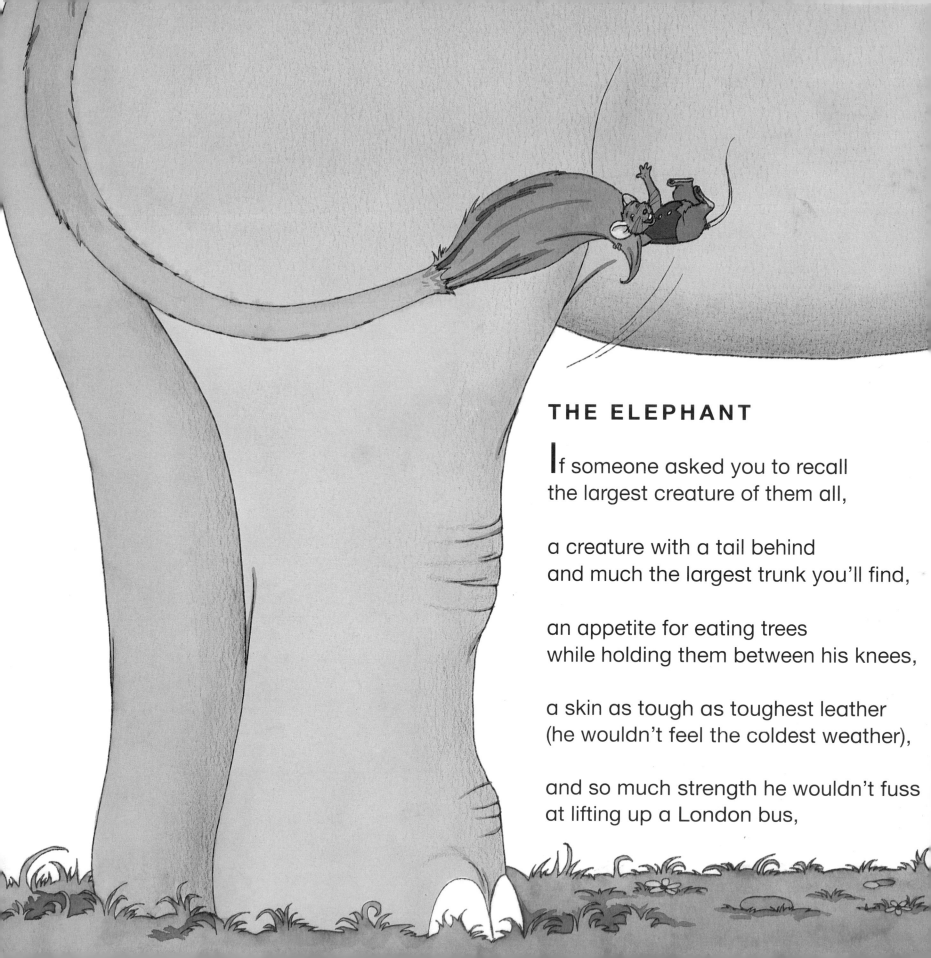

THE ELEPHANT

If someone asked you to recall
the largest creature of them all,

a creature with a tail behind
and much the largest trunk you'll find,

an appetite for eating trees
while holding them between his knees,

a skin as tough as toughest leather
(he wouldn't feel the coldest weather),

and so much strength he wouldn't fuss
at lifting up a London bus,

so big he wouldn't fit inside
a bedroom twenty metres wide,

('cos if he tried, you can be sure
his body wouldn't fit the door),

with such a brain he even knows
to wash behind his ears and toes,

why then, you'll know you're getting ready
to meet an elephant called Eddy.

FIREMAN FRED

He will race up and down
to fight fires in the town
with a speed that's amazing to see.
With a smile on his face
and a hose in its place,
he fights fires wherever they be.

He is kind and he's strong
and he never takes long,
for he's always ready to go,
to fight fires big or small
with flames short or tall.
This Fireman never says "no!"

He's called Fireman Fred
and his engine is red
with a bell that rings out loud and clear.
His ladder goes higher
than the top of a fire
so that Fred can fight fires without fear.

GOLDEN GIRL'S GOAT

Golden Girl has a little grey goat,
who follows wherever she goes.
Whenever she sits in her garden swing,
he comes and nibbles her toes.

Golden Girl's goat eats plenty of grass.
He chews it for hours and hours.
But when Golden Girl isn't looking his way,
he quickly gobbles her flowers.

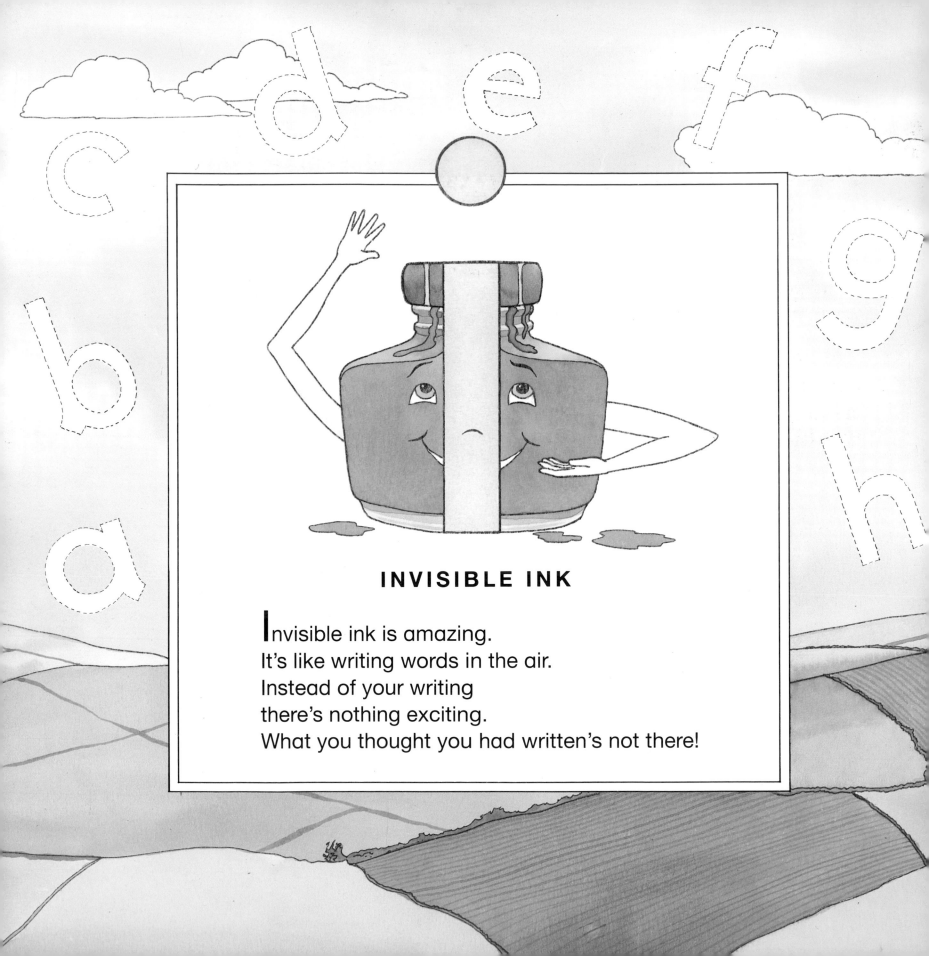

INVISIBLE INK

Invisible ink is amazing.
It's like writing words in the air.
Instead of your writing
there's nothing exciting.
What you thought you had written's not there!

JUMPING IS FUN

Jumping Jim likes jumping.
He says it clears his head.
He always feels much better
when he's just jumped out of bed.

Jumping Jim says jumping
is great for everyone.
It's just as quick as running
and jumping's much more fun.

LETTERLAND FOOTBALL

In Letterland on Saturday
everybody wants to play

a game of kicking with a ball
just inside the castle wall.

The teams are chosen with great care
making sure that they're quite fair.

In Letterland a football game
is even played out in the rain.

The Queen will come in any weather
so long as she has her umbrella.

There's Munching Mike and Jumping Jim
and Sammy Snake who slithers in.

There's Bouncy Ben and Fireman Fred
and sometimes even Robber Red,

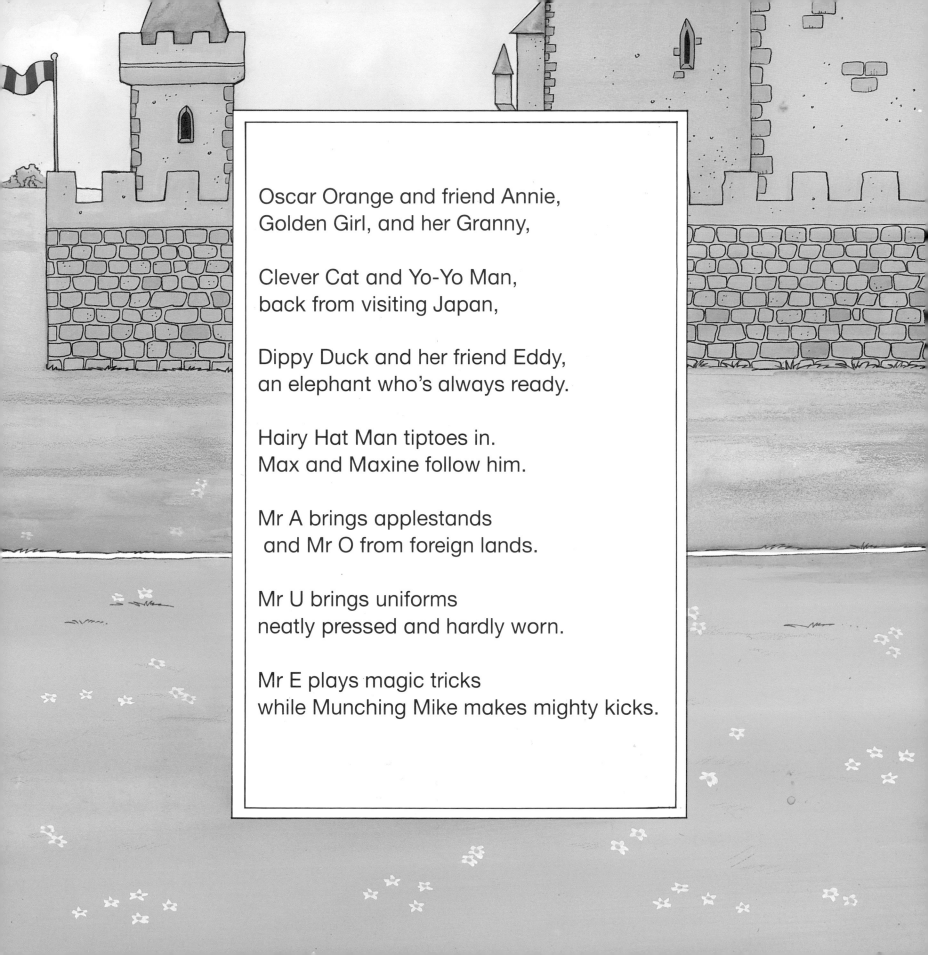

Oscar Orange and friend Annie,
Golden Girl, and her Granny,

Clever Cat and Yo-Yo Man,
back from visiting Japan,

Dippy Duck and her friend Eddy,
an elephant who's always ready.

Hairy Hat Man tiptoes in.
Max and Maxine follow him.

Mr A brings applestands
and Mr O from foreign lands.

Mr U brings uniforms
neatly pressed and hardly worn.

Mr E plays magic tricks
while Munching Mike makes mighty kicks.

Ice-cream's for sale from Mr I
helped by Impy Ink nearby.

Thoughtful Lucy brings a light
in case the game goes on all night.

Naughty Nick brings all his nails
and pins up posters round the rails.

And just in case the air turns nippy
(a dreadful thought for ducks like Dippy)

Oscar Orange and Poor Peter
bring along a water heater!

Vase of Violets makes a show.
See her petals all aglow.

Zig Zag and the Water Witch
race up and down beside the pitch.

Included in this jolly crew
a faithful friend, the kangaroo.

In the cold he wears red mittens,
and brings along two kicking kittens!

There's only one man missing now,
a captain who will show them how

to play the game and kick the ball,
explain the rules and show them all.

In Letterland a football game
just would not, *could* not be the same

without the man they know the best,
who's better far than all the rest.

On Saturdays they roar and sing,
"Here he comes — the Kicking King!"

THE LIGHTHOUSE

The lady who lives in the lighthouse
shines a light you can see for a mile.
It's yellow and bright
and a welcoming sight
when she lights up the night with her smile.

MUNCHING MIKE'S MEAL

Munching Mike

thought a bike

would make a tasty meal.

With one big crunch

and a mighty munch

he munched up all but a wheel.

NICK'S TUMMY

Naughty Nick
took his pick,
counted nine,
said, "They're mine."

Now his tummy's
feeling funny.
Just a tick!
Nick feels sick!

AN ORANGE CALLED OSCAR

The Old Man from over the Ocean
brought oranges over the sea.
His favourite orange was Oscar,
who came from the top of the tree.

In Letterland, Oscar was famous
and everyone wanted to see
what shape and what colour this orange
called Oscar could possibly be.

POOR PETER

Poor Peter's best friend is called Poppy
they look like two peas in a pod.
Their ears are all furry and floppy,
but their patches aren't even, they're odd!

TELL THE QUEEN

Quarrelsome Queen
says, "Have you seen
a forecast of the weather?"

'cos if you do
she says that you
must very quickly tell her.

Quarrelsome Queen
says, "Have you seen
a quill made from a feather?"

'cos if you do
she says that you
must very quickly tell her.

Quarrelsome Queen
says, "Have you seen
my lovely new umbrella?"

'cos if you do
she says that you
must very quickly tell her!

THE ROBBER RASCAL

Robber Red's a rascal.
He races round all day
on roller skates with dinner plates
he's stolen on the way.

Robber Red's a rascal.
He's really quite unable
to eat a roast or slice of toast
before he takes the table!

SAMMY'S SISTER

Sammy Snake in the sand with his sister
played a game called 'squiggle and twister.'
It was like hide-and-seek
and not once did he peek,
so it isn't surprising he missed her.

TICKING TESS

Ticking Tess, in her tower,
can tell you the hour
and the answers to things you should know.
Why the moon looks so sad,
why sometimes we're bad,
and why, for each 'yes', there's a 'no'.

On the phone Ticking Tess
will always say 'yes'
when you ask her, please would she explain
why thunder and lightning
seem to be frightening,
and why we get wet in the rain.

UPPY UMBRELLA

Whatever the weather

if you need an umbrella

then Uppy's the person to call.

If it's rainy or snowy

or sunny or blowy

her umbrella can shelter you all.

VASE OF VIOLETS

My favourite flowers are violets
five petals, a velvety touch.
They grow in high places,
with smiles on their faces,
and a colour I like very much.

WET WASHING

The Water Witch finished her washing
and then she looked up at the sky.
"With this wind and this beautiful sunshine," she said,
"my washing will shortly be dry."

So to reach her washing line better
she jumped to the edge of her letter
but it tipped
and she slipped,
her new woolly ripped
and her washing got wetter and wetter!

MAX'S BIRTHDAY

Max has a birthday tomorrow.
He's six, but he wants to be seven.

For his present he'd like a wheelbarrow
and Wellington boots, size eleven.

THE YELLOW YO-YO MAN

A yo-yo's a toy that you whizz with.
You whirl it and twirl it around.

But there's only one man who can spin it
so it seems to rise up from the ground.

His yo-yos are yellow and shiny.
He even has a yo-yo that glows.

He sings as he spins with his yo-yos
and he takes them wherever he goes.

ZIG ZAG ZOO

Zig Zag Zebra
zoomed around the zoo.
Sammy Snake was snoozing
until Zig Zag woke him too.

Zig Zag Zebra
zoomed around the zoo.
When she finished zooming
Sammy finished too.

Zig Zag Zebra
snoozed in the zoo.
Then Sammy started zooming
and woke up Zig Zag too.

Whizz this way

THE VOWEL MEN

Mr A loves apples
because they're red and round.

Mr E loves magic
and disappearing sounds.

Mr I loves ice cream
because it's very cold.

Mr O the Old Man
loves anything that's old.

Mr U loves uniforms
and playing any games.

But most of all the Vowel Men
love to say their names.

DAYS OF THE WEEK

Munching Mike says Monday
is the best day of the week.

Ticking Tess thinks Tuesday
is best for hide and seek.

The Water Witch on Wednesday
casts her magic spells.

On Thursday, there is thunder
so the rain fills water wells.

Fireman Fred on Friday
fights a fire with foam.

He likes it when it's Saturday
so he can stay at home.

Sammy Snake and Dippy Duck
on Sunday play a game.

While Mr A and Yo-Yo Man
like every day the same.